GITA & NEEL'S STORY (COLLECTION)

A SHORT AND SWEET SERIES

SUDESNA GHOSH

ISBN 979-888546758-2

Contents

One Day in October

PART 1

Durga Puja was finally over. The huge structures made with bamboo poles that blocked every road, were gone. The huge crowds of overdressed people had disappeared. Oh, how much Gita hated the noise, chaos and materialism that came with the annual festival in Kolkata.

"Gita, are you returning to your shop today?"

She nodded, keeping her eyes on her phone. Her father's voice broke into her thoughts again.

"Bring me back some lemon tea cakes this evening, alright?"

"Yes, Baba."

Gita's mother yawned. She was bored. Any talk about Gita or her little cafe was irrelevant to her. The older woman would much rather spend an hour on the phone, chatting with her other daughter, Nita.

Nita was the opposite of Gita. She was slim, always dressed up, and knew that all normal women were meant to get married while their breasts were still perky and their hair still glossy and thick. Nita, was the child who had made her parents happy. She'd made the nosy neighbours happy too. Marrying the perfect man at the age of twenty-five was expected of her. She did them proud when she announced that she was pregnant exactly one year later.

Gita was the black sheep. Older than Nita by four years, she was nowhere near married at twenty-five. And now, at forty-five, she didn't remember how to kiss or even how to go on a date. When she'd hit twenty-five, she broke up with her first and last steady boyfriend, Hemant. He'd been a patronising asshole and didn't help her already low self-esteem.

Twenty years down, Gita loved being on her own and couldn't imagine how Nita lived in her little bubble. Her sister was content with her roles of mother and wife and party organiser – Gita preferred books, cupcakes and the company of two more single female friends.

"Gita," her mother began.

"Yes, Ma?"

"Nita was asking if you'd like to meet their newly divorced friend, Ashok, for dinner tonight?"

Gita sighed. She thought this was over a long time ago.

"Ma, I'm over forty years old. Didn't we agree that you'd stop this after I passed thirty?"

Throwing her shoulder bag over her arm, she didn't wait for a response. Still, her mother wasn't one to let it go. Not ready to take her silence for an answer, she rattled on.

"At the Durga Puja pandal last week, as Nita and I played the Sindoor Khela[1], I saw you crying!"

Gita was speechless. She gripped her bag before it could fall to the floor. Her father pretended to read the paper which he'd already finished an hour ago.

Looking her mother in the eye, she said, "Ma, I don't even like the idea of women marking their foreheads with vermillion or anything else to show they belong to a man."

Her mother frowned. "But I saw you crying," she insisted.

Gita wanted to throw a cake at her mother. It was fortunate that there was no cake nearby that day.

"No. The priest was doing the rituals next to you all, remember? I got teary because of the smoke from the millions of incense sticks, Ma," she rolled her eyes.

Shutting the door behind her, Gita heard her mother call out, "Get me some brownies for tea!"

Getting into her shop, Gita felt her mood improve instantly. Her café was her pride and joy. She had invested all her savings in it a few years ago when she'd been done with the corporate world. The sight of pretty sweet things and the odour of coffee beans pushed her lips into a smile for the first time that day.

She didn't hate her parents. Living with them made sense most of the time with all the space in the house. Plus, she could help them out with errands and doctors' visits. Gita was a dutiful daughter. Nita was too busy with her own family matters and wasn't expected to help in any way. Somehow, being a married woman made her superior in their parents' eyes.

The café door opened. It was Aronie, a regular customer. He always ordered the same thing; a cherries and cream cupcake with a café mocha. In the summer, he opted for iced mochas instead.

Settling into his seat, Aronie asked Gita about her health and Durga Puja festivities. He also suggested that she add outdoor seating to the café. She talked to him until the waiter brought his order to the table.

In a cheerful mood, Aronie wasn't done being chatty. He told her, "Change is a constant but I hate change. I'm happy you understand that here."

"Oh, thank you," she mumbled, not sure what he meant.

Aronie continued, "You see, I visited another café last week and they were irritating me, trying to make me try things I've never tasted before."

Gita understood his feeling too well. In all these years, she had stuck to a set schedule, not breaking away from it even when her mother fell down and broke her leg or when she herself had a fever. Change made her uncomfortable. Structured days gave her comfort.

Biting into his cupcake, Aronie opened his book. He was a bookworm who often spent two hours reading and drinking cup after cup of coffee at the café. Gita had instructed her staff to never hurry him.

A chirpy little voice brought Gita away from the table. "Hello, Gita Aunty!"

It was Shayan from next door. His parents brought him to the café often for hot chocolate.

"Hi Shayan. How are you doing?"

"Aunty, I'm hungry," he moaned as if he hadn't eaten in days.

His mother walked in. She asked for a hot chocolate and two cupcakes. Then she added, "Please give me a mushroom quiche for takeaway."

Gita went to the small office at the back. She needed to check accounts. A week of holidays had messed up her routine. Two hours later, she was done. The only thing left to do that morning was a phone call concerning supplier issues but that wasn't stressing her out. Something else was bothering her. It was her mother's silly allegation.

Gita was used to being compared to her sister since the younger girl was born but when you're over forty years old and independent, you expect some respect. From your loved ones at least. Should she forgive her parents because they were so old?

During Durga Puja, all the neighbours would comment about her spinsterhood until she stopped going to the pandal for more than a quick five-minute viewing of the goddess. Her mother would feel insulted by the gossip mongers and her father would tell them that he had no control over his own daughter. At the end, everyone would conclude that Nita was the good sister.

Over the years, Gita felt her self-esteem dip even with her success at school or at work but it was the café that finally made her feel whole. Today was just a weird day. She could cope. She always did.

"Madam, Nita Madam has come," her staff member came to inform her.

She raised an eyebrow. "Send her in."

[1]Literally meaning 'vermillion game', is a tradition where women smear each other with sindoor on the last day of Durga Puja. Married Bengali Hindu women apply sindoor on the forehead and feet of the goddess and offer sweets to her. Then they put it on each other's faces and offer sweets to each other too.

PART 2

Nita was fuming. Her freshly pedicured feet and hands matched the natural pink on her cheeks. Today was turning out to be a bad day. Gita watched her sister take the chair facing hers. She flipped her hair back and hissed, "Why won't you meet the gentleman we found for you?"

Gita bit her lip. She wanted to ask her when she'd ever asked her to go man searching for her. Taking a deep breath, she answered, "Because I don't want to. And by the way, you have so many parties and trips to organise, so why, oh why, are you wasting so much energy on me?"

Nita didn't get the sarcasm. She barged ahead, "Look, you still look decent at this age. And you can't live like this forever."

Gita stood up, her hands clenching the desk.

"Like *what*, Nita?

"Alone. Childless," she spat out the words, the disgust written all over her perfectly made up face.

Gita had been through this before but it had been a while. She picked up the script again.

"I am happy. I don't like kids. I am not begging you or anyone else for money."

Taking a deep breath, she asked Nita to lower her voice. Her employees and customers didn't need to hear the dirt.

"You want me to meet this man badly it seems. Tell me why."

Nita looked at the wall behind Gita. She didn't meet her eyes. Finally, she muttered, "Ashok is Ravi's cousin."

Ravi was Nita's husband. Nita was the model wife who couldn't say no to her wealthy, controlling spouse. Gita was not getting into this.

She forced herself to smile. "Nita, ask him to find a date using one of those apps that young people use these days."

Now pouting, Nita asked, "You really won't do this for me?"

Gita shook her head, asking her to leave as an important call came in. Shooting her daggers with her big brown eyes, Nita stomped off, leaving a trail of Christian Dior perfume after her.

Rupa was Gita's best friend of ten years. She lived with a cat and a dog. She claimed that no man had ever given her the kind of unconditional love that her pets gave her. Unfortunately, Gita's parents were allergic to pets so she could never adopt one.

Today, Gita was meeting Rupa for an early lunch at the mall. Rupa worked from home but she had an hour to spare.

Seating themselves at the Chinese restaurant, the two friends talked about Durga Puja celebrations and how they avoided the craziness. Gita shared the anecdote about the Sindoor Khela.

"Wow. Your mother really doesn't know you well," she exclaimed.

With a sarcastic laugh, she told Gita about one couple in her neighbourhood who'd gone through a divorce just a year after the big wedding.

"The girl and her family didn't come to the gatherings at all. My other neighbour said they were ashamed."

Gita growled. Patriarchy made her boil. Rupa told her more.

"But you know, the guy and his parents were there all the time. No shame about the marriage ending."

Sipping her mocktail, Gita sighed. Then Rupa went onto more pleasant topics. She wanted to share some news with her as they devoured dim sums. Rupa's eyes lit up as she spoke. Grabbing her friend's hand, she announced, "I'm going to Goa for a week."

Gita knew that her friend couldn't bear to sit in the city for longer than three months at a stretch. She always managed to go away for short vacations. Gita hadn't been on a vacation in years. It would interfere with her daily schedule.

"Hey, you zoned out. I want you to come with me."

"Are you serious?"

"Yes, why not?"

Gita stared at her like she was speaking an unknown language.

"My café needs me. My parents need me. That's why."

Rupa waved off her excuse. "My pets need me. We all have responsibilities but we all deserve a break, Gita!"

Suddenly, her words went straight to Gita's emotional side. She was really overworked and stressed. Plus, she would love a break from her parents and her sister's drama. Maybe she should say yes. The café manager could handle things for a few days. She could call and ask Nita to come by every day to keep an eye on their parents. Daughterly duties weren't just meant for her – even though she'd never say that out loud.

"But what will we do there for a whole week?"

Rupa giggled, "The whole point of a vacation is to not do ANYTHING!"

Gita felt her heart beat faster with anxiety or excitement. She was used to daily to-do lists and the satisfaction of crossing off items throughout the day. She needed a list for Goa. She told Rupa as much and her friend said she'd throw her phone into the water.

Gita realised how silly she sounded. Her friend wanted her to relax and have a good time. So why not? She wondered if she should run the idea by her parents. It wasn't about asking permission but of course, her mother would fuss and say it wasn't safe for single women to travel alone.

Munching on delicious kimchi, Gita made up her mind. She was going. Rupa was ecstatic. But she was worried that Gita would backout at the last moment for fear of leaving her comfort zone. So she had a great idea.

"Hey, let's book your ticket right now. I'll email the hotel about a room for two, okay?"

Gita didn't hesitate when Rupa handed her the phone with the airlines booking page open. She typed in her details and paid for her tickets. Feeling young and impulsive, she did a little happy dance in her chair when the confirmation email came in.

"Goa, here we come!"

The two friends high fived each other, and Gita didn't worry about things for a while. Even though her day had started badly, it was turning out to be fabulous.

After the exciting lunch, Rupa went back home. Gita wasn't needed at the café until the evening. Her manager was doing a great job. Surely, he could manage everything for a week. Looking at her phone for the first time since she'd entered the restaurant, she took a look at her phone calendar. Grocery shopping was scheduled for the next day but she could get it out of the way today. In fact, she was standing a few feet away from the hypermarket. Keeping in mind her parents' favourites, she stocked up her cart. Of course, she had a mental list of items in her head. She put her favourite coffee into the cart as an afterthought. Expensive coffee and eBooks were her weaknesses. She bought several eBooks every weekend for her Kindle device.

Her father called as she was standing in the cashier's line.

"You're coming back soon with the cakes?"

"Yes."

But then she changed her mind. She didn't want to go home directly from the grocery store. Today, she felt different. She called her father back and said she'd be late. She noticed a display board with some cute animals on it. Squinting, she realised it was an ad for the Smurfs movie.

"Hello Baba. I'll come back after my evening visit to the café."

"Where are you?"

She'd expected questions. "Don't worry. I'm safe and happy."

As she said the words, she knew that her father didn't care about happiness. Only corporate success and marital success mattered to him. The man had tormented her until her mid-thirties, taking her from astrologer to astrologer every month. She went along to keep peace at home but later put her foot down. Her father stopped mostly because most of them said she had no marriage on the cards.

Today, Gita wasn't going to feel bad for not rushing home with the goodies that her parents liked. She was also alright with not telling him where she was.

As she stood in line to get her ticket, her mother called too.

"Your father says you're not coming home this afternoon?"

"Yes, I'm not."

"But you always come home by two o' clock," she complained.

Gita firmly said, "Today, I won't."

Ending the call abruptly, Gita tried not to feel guilty. She had a habit of blaming herself for everything and going out of her way to keep her parents happy. Sometimes, she had a nagging feeling that she felt guilty about not living up to their expectations. Well, they had Nita who fulfilled their wishes at least.

PART 3

Gita called the café before she put her phone on silent mode.

"My phone will be on silent for a while. But text me if there is an emergency," she instructed her head of staff.

Her manager was surprised.

"Madam, you told me not to disturb you this afternoon. I promise to take care of everything here. Please don't worry."

But Gita was a worrier. She was used to taking maximum weight on her shoulders. Somehow, taking a break from the usual never hit her mind. Today was different.

"You're right. In fact, I will switch off my phone. See you in the evening," she replied, turning off her device and throwing it into her bag without a second glance.

The usher showed her to her seat. She had a plush Gold Class arm chair. The rest of the theatre was empty. Closing her eyes, she leaned back into the soft cushion, waking up with a jolt seconds later when she reached for water which she'd forgotten to buy. For a change, she could buy iced tea too. Today was for being adventurous. Or adventurous according to her own definition of it.

Sauntering out to the concessions stand, she asked for a bottle of water and a glass of lemon iced tea.

"Madam, no food? No popcorn with that?"

"No. That'll be all," she said, handing him her credit card.

The young man was persistent. He took her card and rattled off the list of popcorn varieties including caramel, cheese, butter and something with berries. Gita was getting impatient. Her cosy seat waited for her.

She gently ended the conversation saying, "I can't eat an entire popcorn by myself. Let it be."

Payment made, she walked back to her spot, feeling bad about saying no. Almost fifty years old but she still sucked at saying no. As her mother sarcastically said once, "Our daughter says yes to everyone but us when we ask her to settle down."

She was compelled to agree on this point. She hated the institution of marriage and had seen enough of affairs and submissive wives including her sister to get herself into that trap. Reclining her seat, Gita placed her bottle on one side and the iced tea on the other. She always enjoyed the solitude. Except for the bad days when she wished for a shoulder and an ear. Then again, she had her loyal friend or two.

"Madam, no popcorn for you?"

Gita sat up straight. The employees at this place were obsessed with popcorn. To make the guy leave her alone, she said, "Yes, give me a caramel one, please."

"Yes, Madam."

"The smallest size."

"Of course, Madam," he eyed the empty seats next to her.

The ads started rolling. Gita mused that she was in a movie theatre after more than a year. It wasn't like she was watching any television or movies at home. Books were much more entertaining in her opinion. The silence intermingled with the words and scenes filling her mind. She loved that precious experience.

Putting popcorn into her mouth, she wondered why kids didn't like watching innocent, sweet things these days. Everything was so dark. Reality was dark enough, wasn't it?

The hall was still empty and the movie was starting. Gita almost checked her phone for messages and missed calls. Almost. She was sipping on water, admiring the blue cute beings on the screen, when she remembered that she had popcorn waiting to be devoured.

Her heart melting at the sweet innocence on the screen, Gita admitted to herself that the popcorn was delicious. The usher interrupted her thought process when he flashed his torch light on her row. There was a young man walking up with a huge tub of popcorn in his hands.

Gita was astonished when he took the seat right next to hers. The ticketing agent must have done that on purpose! Two people in a big hall seated in two adjacent seats. How strange.

She'd stopped checking out men years ago. Most of them were married anyway. This guy sitting next to her would be an exception. Today called for breaking bad habits, so Gita let herself do some healthy gazing.

First of all, they were inside a dark movie theatre with no one else but the usher nearby. Even the usher was far away near the exit. Secondly, they were both fully grown adults watching a kiddie movie. This called for a glance or two. It was too dark for a great view but the interval allowed Gita to stare properly.

He looked about thirty. Dark hair with stylish long locks framed his face. She liked his simple polo neck shirt and jeans look. Nita's husband looked down upon people who wore jeans. He preferred the trousers and full sleeved dress shirt look at all times.

Gita wanted to see this man's face properly; particularly, his eyes. The eyes always gave a look into the soul. Maybe he read her mind because at that moment, her movie companion turned to her. He must have felt her eyes scrutinising him.

"Hi. I'm Neel."

Gathering her composure, Gita felt like a naughty child caught with her hand in the cookie jar. She grinned. "Hi. I'm Gita."

Neel leaned in closer and asked, "So you like the Smurfs too?"

She debated on it. She could tell him the truth about feeling lonely and used but adventurous, or she could pretend to be a Smurfs fan. The semi-truth came out of her mouth, "I like cute movies. No blood or gore. No sad endings. Nothing dark."

Neel smiled a sexy smile. "Me too."

His eyes were bright. They sparkled with wit and warmth. Suddenly, Gita wanted to know more about this stranger. The popcorn guy came by to ask if they wanted to order some more. Neel's tub was untouched. He asked the guy to take it away.

"Why, Sir? You didn't like it?"

Neel frowned and explained, "I asked for caramel but they gave me butter."

Gita felt bad. She also found a good excuse to share more moments with Neel. Her popcorn was only half finished. They generally made them couple sized anyway. So, as the lights went out for the second half of the movie, she whispered, "Hey, you are welcome to share my caramel popcorn with me."

Neel thanked her, popping some into his mouth. They both leaned back into their seats, legs up, relaxed, making Gita wonder why it felt so nice and couple-y. She told herself to stop acting like a romance-starved middle-aged fool.

She felt ridiculous. A forty-five-year-old woman on the start to menopause was instant crushing on a thirty-year-old. In all these years, no man had stirred her hormones. Not even Shah Rukh Khan with his romantic, expressive eyes.

The Smurfs were so cute. Gita had a good laugh when she wasn't distracted by the hot guy sitting next to her. At one point, they both reached into the popcorn tub together, resulting in a gentle touch of flesh. Neel wasn't surprised. Their eyes met, he popped some popcorn into his mouth and winked at her.

When was the last time that a man had winked at her? Over twenty years ago probably.

Gita laughed. Neel most likely thought she was a crazy old lady. First, he caught her staring and then he saw her blushing. But yes, they were both watching a children's movie on a weekday afternoon.

When the movie finished, Neel didn't seem in a hurry to leave. He asked her if he'd seen her before.

"That's an old pickup line," she blurted out.

Immediately, she felt silly. Why would he try any pick up line with someone so much older than him?

"No, I honestly think I've seen you before at a quaint café near my bookstore."

Wait. Gita was intrigued. She may have an addiction to her e-reader, but she often went to Book Palace for paperbacks and stationery.

"You own Book Palace?"

"Yes. Do you own that café?"

She told him that Coffee & Cakes was very much hers. He was wide eyed. They talked about people who came in to read and how she wanted to build a small reading nook inside.

Neel was excited. "I can help you with that for sure."

The usher was waiting for them to leave. Neel put out a hand even though Gita didn't need any help getting up. Maybe he thought she was really old and had movement issues already. They stepped out the doors and he asked her if she was in a hurry.

"I have some time."

"Do you feel like I do right now?"

She was confused. Neel stopped walking and stood in front of her.

"Do you feel happy, stress free and kind of like a child?"

Oh wow. He was so right. That described her current state perfectly. She hadn't felt this way in years. She did remind him that she was over forty years old. He brushed it off saying she looked happy today.

"When you look happy, you look beautiful, Gita. No matter how old you are," he told her. He was intense. Not like most of the young guys Gita saw at the café. She felt the blushing start again. Neel was so sweet. Or maybe he was just being polite and nothing else.

Thanking him, she started walking towards the exit. He was still by her side.

"Gita, I think the movie gods wanted us to meet today," he said seriously.

She realised that he was talking about fate. It didn't sound cheesy. There was nothing cheesy about Neel. He clearly spoke from the heart. He continued, "They even put us in A5 and A6."

Neel offered her his hand and asked, "Can we let this feeling linger a little longer? Can I get us ice cream from the old man's cart outside?"

Gita took his hand. It felt right. They left the mall and he got her ice cream. Gita didn't remember the last time she'd bought ice cream from anywhere but the grocery store or mall food court. Taking their cones, they licked their ice cream and laughed all the way to Coffee & Cakes.

Gita learned about Neel and he learned about her. Her phone was still off. They walked along with couples and groups of people. They passed by office employees grabbing lunch at the roadside stalls. But they saw nothing but each other. By the time they'd reached the café, they had exchanged phone numbers.

For a minute, Gita hoped that her staff wouldn't label her a cougar. But in the next minute, she didn't care. People labelled people all the time no matter what they did or didn't do. She was okay with going from old spinster to cougar.

Before he said goodbye, Neel gave her hand a squeeze.

"I promise to take you to a fancier date next time," he said.

"Popcorn and ice cream weren't so bad," she answered, winking at him now.

She told him that it was the best day and the best date that she'd ever had.

THE END

One Night in November

PART 1

"Hey, beautiful."

She turned around, landing in his outstretched arms. Neel was at her café, waiting to take her home for their movie date.

"I missed you," he declared, coming in for a quick kiss.

Gita grinned, reminding him that they'd met just a few hours ago. At tea time.

Pouting, he complained, "But that was hours ago!"

She pulled him into a slow kiss. She had become quite the daredevil since they'd met six weeks ago. Kissing in her little back office at her own café was normal now. She loved the scandalous vibe she felt every time he walked in and the staff nodded at him politely.

"Did you get the Bengali books that I ordered for my father?"

Neel nodded, handing her the bag full of books. Neel's bookstore was her second home now, after the café of course.

That afternoon, they'd chatted over lattes and lemon cake. By now, her employees knew where she was going every afternoon. Her parents were curious too at the sudden change in routine. They asked her if she was eating at the café or up to something else that they should know about.

"Have you opened a new café?" Her father was hopeful. He loved the constant supply of goodies.

Gita wished she had the money but there was the small nook at Neel's store that they were planning to convert into a cosy coffee corner. She looked forward to that.

"Are you meeting friends for lunch every day?" Her mother asked this time.

Gita said yes, hoping they were done.

Her mother wouldn't let go. She continued, "But your friend comes to meet you like this and her boss doesn't mind? Or she has her own business like you?"

Sighing, Gita responded, "Ma, my friend owns a bookstore. And everyone deserves a lunch break if they're their own boss or not, right?"

The older woman rolled her eyes. She wasn't done.

"At your age, people usually find themselves busy raising children and maintaining a house and husband."

It never stopped. No matter how old she got. No matter how clear she'd made her stance on the path that society prescribed for women.

"Ma, we agreed that I'm too old for this sort of conversation."

Her mother sighed, shifting her attention to her phone where her other daughter had sent her pictures of her latest sari buying spree. Gita would rather that her mother stay busy with that than pick on every aspect of her life.

But Gita's father had something to say.

"It's good to see you meeting friends for lunch."

She knew there would be more. She waited with bated breath.

"Too bad you never met any boys for lunch when you were young and pretty."

The obsession with marriage would never end in her house.

Today, Neel and Gita were planning to snuggle on his couch with a chick flick for company. Neel loved sweet, happy endings as much as she did. Gita enjoyed lying down with her head on his lap, looking up at him and finding him watching her. Sometimes that led to a major make out session and at other times it led to the best sex that Gita had had in her forty something years.

The first time, she'd been shy and worried about cellulite and her generous curves, but then Neel had made her feel like the most desirable woman on earth. In fact, he always made her feel special when they were together. Even if they were communicating by phone, he was focused on her and she knew it.

"Hey. Food first or sex first?"

Neel was to-the-point as usual.

Gita pretended to think about it, driving him crazy as she stalled. He pretended to lose interest, walking off to the bedroom without looking back once. Gita ran after him like a naughty teen, shouting, "Sex first!"

Neel was waiting for her, naked. Gita pulled off her own clothes and joined him. The movie and the food could wait.

By the time she got home, it was nine o' clock. Her parents were in front of the TV, the news blasting at full volume. Of course, they refused to wear their hearing aids. Gita had purchased the best for them a year ago. They were sitting in the drawer.

"Your friend had dinner with you today?"

"Yes, Ma. We ate dinner together."

Heading to her room, Gita heard her father ask, "At your café?"

"No, Baba. At his house."

The moment the word 'his' came out of her mouth, Gita knew she was going to face the Spanish Inquisition.

"Goodnight," she told them, closing the door.

She knew it was silly. She wasn't an underage school girl who should worry about her parents finding out about a boyfriend. She gave a damn about what strangers thought about her but her brain worked differently when it came to her folks.

As she let the shower warm her up, Gita remembered how Neel had held her that night. She remembered how he hadn't wanted her to leave. At her age, she couldn't stay the night at her lover's place because it would cause drama at home—especially if they found out that he was significantly younger than her.

Neel had texted her goodnight. They hadn't used the L-word yet but Gita knew she was there. The last six weeks had been life changing since they'd met at the movie theatre. Neel and Gita were inseparable. They couldn't get enough of each other and it was beautiful, instant chemistry both mentally and physically.

Gita was happy and she had learned to relax and enjoy moments for herself. After years of only thinking about others' needs, she was feeling like a new person. Plus, it didn't hurt that Neel was hot. He looked like a young, Indian version of George Clooney.

As she smiled, he sent her a music video. It was the classic *I can't help falling in love with you*. She was too exhausted to type, sending him a heart emoji and drifting into sweet dreams.

PART 2

Gita woke up with beads of sweat on her forehead. She realised that the ceiling fan wasn't moving. All winter long, she loved using a thick blanket with the breeze of the fan surrounding her too. Outside, it was pitch dark. That could only mean one thing – a dreaded power outage. The occasional power cut wasn't uncommon in Kolkata and the apartment complex had a generator that usually brought back the fans and lights in minutes.

"The electricity is gone," her father shouted through the door.

Her mother knocked a second later and yelled, "Come out with your torch."

Gita didn't want to go out. She would have to sit on the balcony with them and answer query after query. Still, she got up, turning on her phone torch light as she opened her door.

Her parents were thanking their stars.

"Imagine if this happened in the summer," they said.

Kolkata was terribly humid and hot most of the year so yes, November was a better time to be without fans and air conditioning. But the darkness was unsettling. Gita kept a small light on even when she slept. Without it, she didn't feel safe.

Her phone was low on charge. She hadn't replied to Neel earlier but she was fully alert now, so she texted him.

I'm falling in love with you too.

Electricity gone. Phone low on charge. Switching off for a bit.

Her father called the neighbourhood electrician. "Son, when will you turn the generator on?"

He frowned at the reply, saying, "How ridiculous!"

When he ended the call, Gita asked, "What happened?"

"Sudeep said that the generator isn't working. The building authorities don't care."

Gita groaned. Her mother seemed unperturbed. She took the opportunity to ask, "Gita, you never told us whose house you had dinner at. You have a new friend of the opposite sex suddenly?"

She bit her lip. It was going to be a long night.

She was old enough to go places without informing them, yet Gita's parents still made her feel like a teen sometimes.

"Ma, you keep wishing that I was married but then you act like meeting a man for a meal is a crime," she shot back, her eyes fixed on the beautiful moon.

Her mother made a noise. It was a rude sound that Gita was used to. People never changed; she realised that after living with her parents for decades.

Her father asked if the man was from a good family. He reminded her about her perfect sister. "Your sister married well. Is your boyfriend well-established? What was his father's profession? Who was his grandfather?"

Gita observed her pale pink fingernails. She had made time for a manicure and pedicure that week. Maybe next time she'd try a risque red. Still calm, she spoke, "Baba, my friend is a kind gentleman and we haven't discussed his family background."

Gasping, her mother looked as if she'd been slapped. The drama was nothing unusual at their house. Gita decided to leave them for a bit, finding her way to the candles in the living room cupboard. They were vanilla and cinnamon candles that she'd picked up during her Diwali shopping. Her parents hadn't approved, asking her if such expensive candles were necessary.

Back on the balcony, she placed two candles on either side of them.

Glaring at the candles, her mother accused, "You are spending so much money these days."

Gita fought with her tongue. She was dying to get back to the privacy of her room. On his phone, her father checked the local news updates and the neighbourhood chat group. The power grid had collapsed in their area and the electricity wouldn't be back till the afternoon. The men would be working all night.

"Gita, are you dating a divorcee?" She leaned forward, eager to know more. If she got anything interesting, her other daughter would be updated by phone first thing in the morning.

"No, Ma. But even if I did, it doesn't matter because I'm past marriageable age anyway, right?"

She winked, getting her ebook reader from the living room coffee table. It was almost fully charged and thank goodness for the built-in light. Reading could help her deal with the night.

The parents exchanged glances as she sat down on the ottoman, throwing her attention to her device. It was a romance novel full of sex and hope – the perfect antidote to the current situation. Neel was probably fast asleep by now, his current read resting on his broad chest. He fell asleep reading most nights.

"When you spend the night with me, we can read together in bed," he'd told her once.

She hoped that would happen someday soon. Tonight, she'd have to read alone and filter out the toxic parents and the lack of fan and light. Tonight was not going to be an easy night for sure.

At one o'clock, her parents were snoring in half-sitting positions. They were all still on the balcony and the only light present was from her candles and the moon. Gita yawned. Her eyes were tired. She put her ebook reader down and checked her phone for messages. There was a text from Neel from half an hour ago. He was worried about her. He hoped she had enough candles to take her through the night. Gita texted back saying she missed him. It turned out that he was awake as he responded in a second:

I'm coming to get you.

Gita was confused. He was well aware that she lived with two difficult beings. Plus, it was so late in the night. He must have been joking.

PART 3

The candlelight gave her solace. It brought some warmth despite the chilly tones used by her parents. These days, her tone was picking up their sarcastic, nasty style too. She hated hearing herself and was not in the mood for any small talk with them. Her relationship with them was not about normal conversations and chit-chat.

"Let's have some biscuits," her mother suggested.

Gita took the cue to bring over the tin of dark chocolate biscuits from her café. It was an odd time to eat and she longed for a cup of coffee to accompany her snack but she couldn't bring herself to do it. Sleep was pulling at her eyes.

Munching on a biscuit, her father asked, "Did you stop making those delicious ginger cookies?"

"No, Baba. They're always available. I'll bring some tomorrow. I mean, later today."

Her mother fanned herself with a newspaper. Her father did the same. It was November but the whole family was used to having the fans running all day and night.

"Oh no! I stretched my neck," her mother moaned, throwing down the newspaper.

Gita stood up, planting herself behind her mother, starting to massage her neck lightly. She had an idea.

"Ma, I'll go get the pain relief gel."

Her father told her to hurry up. In his opinion, they had an emergency. He handed her the torch, leaning back with his arms crossed across his chest. When she returned to the balcony with the gel, he was snoring. The sound cut through the silence in a creepy way. Gita wanted to shout at the electricity company.

She was barely done spreading the gel on her mother's neck and shoulders when someone knocked on their door. The door bell was dead with the current gone. There was a second knock. It was done with urgency. The little hairs on Gita's neck stood up. Her parents locked eyes with her, their eyes wide. Then the third knock sent them into action.

"Let me call the police," her father whispered.

His phone had run out of charge.

"Let's lock ourselves into the bedroom." her other parent suggested.

Gita took a deep breath. She exhaled and went to the door with her phone torch on. On tiptoe, she flashed it at the peephole. It was completely black outside on the landing so she saw nothing. No, wait. She noticed a flicker of candle light.

Her parents stood arm in arm, admiring her for once. They thought she was being brave and their protector. She called out, "Who is it?"

A familiar voice replied, "Gita. It's me."

Coming forward, her father stared at her. He wanted to know, "Who was 'me'?"

She couldn't help it. She had to giggle. She was so glad and so petrified at the same time. The voice belonged to Neel. Her parents were going to meet the love of her life at the oddest hour and in the oddest of ways.

She turned to the elders and told them it was her friend. "Neel must have come to check on us."

She was braless and in old cotton shorts and tee but he'd seen all of her so it wouldn't matter. She hoped he wouldn't hug her in front of them. He always hugged her and held her close whenever he could. She loved that. It was her safe space. Her happy space.

Neel walked in with his candle. He was wearing shorts and tee too. Her parents looked like they were about to faint. The sweet cinnamon smell from his candle hit their noses. Face lit up because he was so happy to see her and because of the flame, Neel looked at her as if no one else was in the room.

Gita quickly pointed her torch at her curious parents. The light made their disapproving facial expressions come into focus. Even if they didn't like the thought of this young man as a potential son-in-law, they wanted to be introduced to him.

"Ma. Baba. This is my friend Neel."

Neel said hello, the flame flickering as he followed them to the balcony. Speechless for a while, Gita let her mother bombard him with her queries. To Neel's credit, he answered her politely while stealing occasional glances at Gita.

"Young man, isn't it rather late for a visit to a friend's house?"

Her father could be rude but his question was valid at that hour. Neel apologised. He admitted that he was worried about Gita and came over to drive them all to his place for the night. They'd have electricity and comfort there.

"I thought you all could come and get a good night's sleep at my place," he offered.

Then he made the error of adding, "I know Gita always needs a fan and light on even in the cold weather."

Oops! Gita almost threw a potted plant at him. In six weeks, he knew her well. Her parents didn't need to know that.

Her father raised an eyebrow. "How long have you known my daughter?"

Gita jumped in. "A few months."

"Oh."

Giving Neel his evilest eye, her father announced, "We don't wish to go anywhere. Thank you for the offer."

Her mother nodded. Neel said, "I understand, Sir."

Facing Gita, he asked, "What about you?"

The older man in the room barked, "What about her?"

Suddenly, Gita was furious. Her father could not interfere like this. She was not going to allow it. Raising her chin, she ignored him. Neel was looking at her and only at her. The intensity in his eyes magnified by the candle light.

"Yes, Neel. I'll come with you. Let me get my phone charger and things."

Her parents followed her to her room. Neel followed them. It was awkward.

"You cannot go stay at a man's house like this!"

Through gritted teeth she replied, "Ma, I am sweating here and we can't even turn on the mosquito repellent."

"He's half your age," her father countered.

"No, he is not, Baba. And even if he was, I don't care."

Then her mother interjected, "What will people say, Gita?"

Gita packed her belongings into a shoulder bag, looked her mother in the eye and said, "I am too old for this."

Hoping to stop the scandalous incident from happening, her father resorted to putting her down as usual. "You couldn't find someone your own age when you finally managed to find someone?"

It felt like a slap. Gita didn't let him see that she was wounded. Instead, she walked to the main door with Neel at her heels.

"Good girls don't spend the night at random boys' houses," her mother warned.

"Well, Ma. I'm not a good girl. In fact, I am a grown woman who has been too good to you all these years for nothing good in return," she spat out.

Neel was holding her hand now. The candle in his other hand. Her heart was beating fast but she was glad to get some of the pent up anger out. They were too used to one-sided mental abuse.

"You should stay and look after us," her father attempted emotional blackmail.

She had done enough of that. For years. It had earned her no respect or love. Her sister on the other hand, had their parents' respect and support just because she was married and with children and leading the life that Gita had not chosen for herself.

Gita was entitled to lead her own life in her own way. Before she walked out, she told them she'd be back soon.

"Not after you have sex with a boy you aren't even engaged to!"

Her mother's beautiful features were looking nasty in the darkness. Maybe even scary. Gita let Neel hold her close by the waist as she retorted, "Sex can happen at any hour of the day, Ma! And it's time I move out anyway."

The older woman's mouth dropped open. Her father slammed the door.Neel held his candle for her, leading her to his car. Once inside it, she burst into tears, letting herself sink into the assurance of his arms.

It was time for a fresh start.

PART 4

Gita slept in his arms until the doorbell rang a few hours later. They sat up, both fully clothed but with eyes that were struggling to stay open. Neel got up first, running his fingers through his hair as he wondered who it was.

"Is it your household help? Or maybe the newspaper guy?" Gita yawned.

Neel shook his head, saying the help came much later in the day. Also, he reminded her that he read all his news online. Newspapers didn't come to his house. When the doorbell rang again, he gently helped her out of bed.

"You sit on the sofa while I go see who it is, okay?"

She agreed, still half awake and longing to get back under the covers until the cafe staff called to find out where she'd disappeared to. She guessed that Neel didn't want anyone to know they'd spent the night in his bed if the person walked in. She knew that his parents lived in Delhi. His small circle of friends would never wake up so early for a visit. Maybe it was the garbage collector?

Familiar voices cut into her thoughts. The people ringing the doorbell at this early hour were her parents. They had found her somehow. She wanted to know how. But first, her mother wanted to say sorry. It was a word that Gita had never heard her use before.

"I am a terrible mother. Please come home. I'm sorry I'm nicer to your sister."

Gita pinched herself. Was this a dream? She watched her mother sit down on the sofa, keeping a healthy distance between them, while her father cleared his throat. He had something to say as well.

"Your mother and I should have been more understanding last night," he admitted, staring at his toes.

Neel asked him to sit down, rushing to the kitchen to make tea and coffee for everyone. He was a good person and no matter how unhappy Gita's parents made her, he knew that she loved them. Her love didn't come from a sense of duty; it was straight from her heart.

Gita wanted to say thanks for the apology and go back to sleep. Last night had been a long, exhausting night. She wanted to turn the fan on full speed and light a de-stressing lavender candle when she felt more alert. Unfortunately, her parents didn't look like they were leaving anytime soon. Both of them accepted tea and biscuits from Neel, maintaining an uncanny silence. Very unlike them.

She sipped her coffee. Neel busied himself cutting fruits at the dining table, giving them their space. At last, Gita asked, "How did you find Neel's house?"

They looked sheepishly at each other. Her mother hid her face in her cup, murmuring inside it. Her father gestured at Neel.

"This wonderful young man left his name, address and phone number on the balcony last night. He knew we'd be worried. Your mother saw it right after you left."

Wow. Neel was so thoughtful. He really cared. So much for all the talk about younger men being irresponsible and unreliable and wild. Neel had acted in a very mature way that night. He was a real keeper.

Before she could ask them to apologise to Neel, he brought in a plate of fruit, asking everyone to help themselves. The fruit was arranged like one of those breakfast buffet platters at star hotels. Gita appreciated his sense of aesthetics. Her mother echoed the thought.

"Young man! This looks beautiful. And you did it so fast," she complimented.

Her father put a grape in his mouth, chewing slowly. He was almost ready to say sorry. Gita chewed on pomegranate while she waited. Her mother asked Neel if his mother had taught him how to cut fruit so nicely.

"My grandmother taught me. She taught me how to cook too."

Gita was done waiting. "Baba and Ma. Don't you think you owe someone else an apology?"

Putting his fork down, her father walked over to Neel, placing a hand on his shoulder. Neel did not fidget.

"Neel, you are a kind-hearted person and we are happy to have you in our lives."

Gita asked him about the missing word that started with an 's'. She needed to hear it to know that he meant it.

"I'm sorry. So is Gita's mother."

Neel accepted the apology and said he would drop them all home. However, Gita said she would go straight to the cafe. Her bag contained a change of clothes among other items. Although her mother opened her mouth to say something, she closed it when her husband touched her lightly on the arm. He asked her if she would come back home.

She smiled. "Yes, I will. With ginger cookies."

Neel squeezed her hand. He was relieved. Whispering into her ear, he asked her if she was angry about him leaving the note for her parents. She wasn't. She'd been angry. Her parents were old and imperfect but Neel had done the right thing. She was so happy that this man standing next to her loved her so much.

Kissing his cheek, she whispered, "You did the right thing. Thank you."

Getting his car keys, he took the older couple to his car, chatting all the way about his bookstore and the history of his building. Her father loved making connections and networking so by the time Neel had started the car, he'd figured out that Neel's paternal uncle was his college junior. The couple was so intrigued by Neel's knowledge of local history that they never even asked him how old he was.

THE END

One Evening in December

PART 1

Christmas Eve was always busy. The cafe closed early after delivering orders and greeting customers all day. Festive cakes and hot chocolate were in high demand. The Christmas tree stood tall near the shelf displaying gingerbread houses.

Gita loved Christmas. It was her favourite holiday. Unlike Durga Puja and Diwali, the year end was more about peace, delicious cake, and small, close knit gatherings. Even her parents seemed to be full of love and kindness and uncharacteristic warmth during this time of the year.

Gita was excited about spending Christmas Eve evening with them because Neel would be joining them. Oh, and her sister. Nita wasn't bringing the kids along because they would be busy meeting friends and getting ready for a party at their parents' club later that evening. Gita's brother-in-law was out of town for work but due back that night. Gita had never got good vibes from the man. He was pretentious and patriarchal. She didn't like him and the feeling was reciprocated from his side.

"Do we need a mistletoe?"

Neel's voice broke into her thoughts. She turned around after giving one last glance at the pretty cakes.

"No, we don't but we need to get a room. Right now," she winked, leading the way to her little office at the back.

Closing the door, Gita let him grab her in his arms. After a long, tender kiss, she said, "Okay, I need to breathe now."

Neel chuckled, handing her a nicely wrapped gift box.

"Wait. Let me fix my lipstick and I'll open it before everyone arrives," she said.

He touched her hand.

"No. Open it after they leave please," he requested, his eyes serious.

She agreed, wondering if the box contained something that could shock her family. Like a sex toy maybe? Or lingerie? It was obviously something good and worth waiting for.

Neel half joked and asked, "So what time is your sister coming? I'm dying to meet her."

Biting her lip, Gita answered, "Please don't be offended if she's rude. She's rude to almost everyone."

Neel rolled his eyes. "For you, I'll tolerate anything," he declared.

Grinning, Gita went back outside to check on the closing routine. Her staff had just put up the 'Closed' sign at the door. The lights were dimmed. Tiny fairy lights and a lamp glowed.

"Go home, please. And Merry Christmas," Gita told her employees.

The staff thanked her, leaving with their carefully put together gift hampers of cakes and cookies for their families. Gita was generous on all holidays but especially on Christmas.

Door locked from the inside, Gita called her parents to ask them if they were running late.

"No, your mother couldn't decide on a sari until ten minutes ago," her father complained.

Her mother came on the line. "Gita, we'll be there in ten minutes." She paused.

"Has the boy arrived?"

Gita smiled at the phone.

"Ma, he has come. Nita will come soon too. And please stop calling him a boy."

Her mother gasped, ignoring the last line.

"You've invited her?"

Gita smirked. She asked her mother to hurry up and come over to the cafe.

Back inside the office, Gita eyed her gift box as Neel checked his emails.

"It'll be worth the wait. I promise," he told her, putting his phone down when she gave him an exaggerated pout.

"Fine. Then you can't open your gift until then too."

Neel agreed. She had got him his favourite coffee beans and festive mugs. Neel loved his coffee.

Eyes looking deep into her, he said, "I love you."

Gita melted. "I know that. But I think you love your coffee more."

With fake surprise and indignation, Neel jumped up to protest. He said he wouldn't kiss her until she said she loved him too. Gita couldn't handle that sort of punishment, so she giggled and gave in.

"You know I love you too."

Neel collapsed dramatically on his chair, sipping water before exhaling. Gita raised an eyebrow.

"You're as dramatic as my family members."

He held his chin up. "And that's why I'm perfect for you, right?"

The phone rang. Gita's parents had arrived. They were feeling cold outside since they'd arrived sixty seconds ago. Her mother claimed to be getting frost bite.

"I'm coming," Gita replied, running to the door. Neel stayed inside. He would let them spend some family time together first. Fortunately, Gita's parents liked him after they'd met him last month.

They hadn't met him again after that one night in November but Neel knew that they asked about him without expressing much disapproval. He was in love and Gita's parents couldn't change that even if they tried. Neel and Gita both relished the idea of love and loyalty rather than the social construct involving rings and paperwork. They both enjoyed every moment together without wanting anything more.

"Sit down and I'll get the hot chocolate," Gita instructed, walking toward the kitchen.

Neel would want coffee. She would get that for him later. Or he knew he could enter the kitchen and make it himself. Neel was good in the kitchen.

Admiring the Christmas tree, Gita's mother shouted out, "This tree must have cost a fortune!"

Gita pretended not to hear. She wouldn't let anyone ruin her festive mood. Back with the mugs of hot cocoa, she left her parents alone again to get the baked goodies. She was happy that her father appreciated the cafe cookies and cakes so much. Throughout the year, she supplied him with his favourites and they never ordered in desserts from anywhere else.

Placing the tray in front of them, she took a seat.

"Where is your sister?"

Her mother would do this every five minutes until her favourite daughter showed up. Gita called Nita and handed the phone to her mother without a word.

The older woman demanded to know, "Where are you? We are waiting for you."

Gita's father was not listening. He was savouring every bite and sip. Gita chose a Santa cookie for herself, wondering if her mother noticed her presence at all.

Phone call done, her mother got straight to the point. "Where's the young boy?"

Gripping her glass, Gita reminded her mother that Neel was a fully grown man. An adult. She pleaded, "Please don't call him a boy when you see him, Ma."

Her father asked if the hot chocolate was imported. He liked fancy things.

"No, Baba. But the mug is from my friend's shop in Singapore."

He approved with a little grunt, leaning back in his chair. Chewing slowly, her eyes darting to and fro, Gita's mother finally asked, "You said he's here. Why can't we see him?"

"Ma, he's finishing some work in my office."

Confused, her mother responded, "But he runs a book store."

"Ma, business owners have to keep track of sales and every day matters. What do you think I do here?"

Wide-eyed, her mother said, "I thought you make and serve food and coffee all day."

Her father pitched in then, "Yes, why do you need to waste money hiring so many people when you can do it yourself?"

Gita stayed calm. She counted to ten in her head,

planning to switch the topic of conversation. Before she could do that, Neel came out.

PART 2

"Hello, young man! Nice to see you again."

Gita's father used the tone he would use to speak to a child. Gita hoped that he wouldn't pat Neel on the head and pull his cheek too. Thankfully, he didn't do either of those things. Neel said hello to her mother who was calling Nita again to see why she was late. So rude, thought Gita.

"Ma, Neel just said hello to you."

The older woman put her phone down, squinting at Neel through her glasses. She managed to smile without looking him up and down.

"Hello little...umm, sorry, young man," she mumbled.

Neel stuck his tongue out at Gita, taking the chair next to her father's. He appeared to be at ease, not reflecting the anxious butterflies in Gita's body. Ever since they'd met, Gita admired this quality in him. Neel never got worked up about anything. He was chilled out at all times. Like even when his bookstore employee stole a bag of books last month.

Suddenly perked up, her mother ordered, "Gita, go make him some hot chocolate."

Neel stopped her. He did not think that the woman of the house or the relationship was supposed to do all the kitchen related chores.

"It's okay, Aunty. I'll make the hot chocolate and coffee myself. Don't worry."

Gita's mother was stunned. She couldn't let her daughter behave this way. It embarrassed her. So she tried again. "Gita, that doesn't look nice. Go make it now."

Gita didn't move. Neel locked eyes with her, got up and went to the kitchen so the matter could be settled without more wasted words. As he stepped away, Gita's father told his wife to stop interfering.

"Boys today are different. Let them be."

This was new. Gita felt her heart flutter. She hadn't expected this. Her father was big on patriarchy. Maybe that one night in November had affected his mindset more than she'd thought.

She asked her parents if they liked the cakes and cookies spread out on the table. Her father nodded, still chewing. Her mother commented, "It's all tasty. We can't eat any sweet things for a month after this."

Gita knew her parents loved sweets. Their collective sweet tooth was a major one. The old couple would be asking for goodies from her cafe within a few days. But she stayed quiet. Her mother could be touchy about her dessert consumption and weight related topics.

Neel was still in the kitchen, perhaps planning to hide until Gita's family left. Just as she got up to check on him, Nita breezed in.

The sisters were a sharp contrast both inside and out. While Gita wore a long skirt with a scoop necked long sleeved top and only earrings as accessories, Nita wore a designer sari that may have been glowing in the dim lighting. On her ear and wrists were crystals including a limited edition watch.

Their mother and father inspected Nita's display with pride. Nita really knew how to dress up. She was leading the right kind of life. The parents were happy and so were the neighbours. Gita was in an undefined relationship with a younger man -- she couldn't be more different from her sister.

"Hi. Thanks for coming," she said with genuine enthusiasm, hugging her sister.

Nita handed her a gift. She handed gifts to their parents too. Gita would be taking her gifts over to them in the morning after wrapping them at Neel's house. Thanking Nita, she made a mental note to order a gift for her sister. It would be a late gift. She'd invited her at the last minute. A gift had escaped her mind.

Nita surveyed the cafe with a critical eye. She and her husband and children were used to five star venues for their coffee dates and get-togethers. Lips turned down, she asked, "Where's your boyfriend?"

"He's making coffee. Would you like some? Or hot chocolate?"

Nita asked for coffee. Black. She watched her weight. Gita was alright with love handles and a large bottom. She was also relieved to leave the room for a bit. Neel pecked her lips as she walked into the kitchen, tucking a strand of hair behind her ear. He was enjoying this. His own parents were far away at a hill station for a phones-free vacation. They hadn't met Gita yet. But then again, things were moving fast and marriage and engagement were the real reasons to meet the parents in India. Serious relationships were supposed to culminate in wedded bliss. Gita and Neel didn't believe that.

"Come out with the coffee. Oh, Nita wants a black coffee. She's here."

"Are you sure Nita won't call me an immature boy again like she did in that text to your mother?"

Gita cringed. She had seen the message when her mother had shown her a picture below it. A picture of her favourite daughter's new gold earrings.

"Well, if she does, we won't give her any cake," she replied.

Neel laughed, touching her nose with his. It was a gesture that reminded Gita how much affection she'd felt and received since they'd met that one day in October. Neel and her had just clicked. Fate had happened. She felt like they'd been together for years. In a good way, of course.

Coffee tray in his hands, water glasses in hers, they made their way to the family. Nita raised an eyebrow at Neel. She'd never seen a man of the house carry a tray before.

"Gita, where are your staff? Why are you both doing all this menial work?"

Nita was quite class conscious and unkind. Gita told her that no work was menial, putting her coffee down in front of her. Neel didn't say hello to her. He let her begin.

"So you're the cutie my big sister is having fun with."

Sitting down across from her, Neel put his hand forward for a shake. Nita was probably expecting air kisses while being cheek-to-cheek. Gita had no idea how those were done. Neither did Neel.

Shaking his hand in a ladylike way, Nita asked, "Oh, I forgot. How old are you again?"

Neel looked at Gita, who fake smiled at her rude sibling and responded on his behalf, "He's sweet sixteen."

Nita made a comment about disliking sarcasm. Gita said she hated rude blood relatives. It could have been a huge showdown if their father hadn't interrupted.

He cleared his throat and enquired, "So what did you study in college?"

Gita had a face palm moment. "Baba, that was ages ago."

Neel deadpanned, "I don't even think I remember, to be honest."

Nita almost fell off her chair. She asked him if he was college educated at all.

"Yes, Ma'am. I studied engineering."

Neel was being quite polite considering the situation. Gita decided to throw a question at her sister then.

"Did you know that Neel has a masters from Cornell?"

Nita was dumbstruck. She'd never heard of Cornell University. So their father pitched in. "It's a top university in America, dear."

Neel asked the old folks if they'd like more hot chocolate. Gita's father said yes. This time Gita went to get it, leaving poor Neel with her weird family. Nita really pissed her off. Not surprisingly, her kids were as rude as her. Her husband hardly spoke to Gita and her parents and rarely met them too. Gita rated kindness number one on her list of priorities and her sister was at zero.

Hot chocolate mugs filled to the brim, she returned to the family and Neel. Nita and her mother were discussing Nita's fancy Christmas lunch plans. Her husband was returning soon and expected her to organise a grand event as always.

"What did he give you for Christmas?"

"Ma, he gives me nice things even without an occasion," Nita replied, wagging a diamond clad finger at her mother and sister.

The males were talking about books and the current political climate in the country. Gita's father was astonished when Neel said, "I've been to England just to visit all the great authors' houses. Jane Austen, Shakespeare and the others. It was on my bucket list for my twenties."

That put Gita's mother back into action. She asked him, "Do you know how to read Bengali?"

"Yes, I can read in Bengali, English, French, and Hindi."

The older male was impressed. Then not missing a beat, he sighed, "Gita can only read in two languages. English and Bengali."

Gita smirked. At least they thought he was smarter than her. The obsession with their age gap could be forgotten. For a few minutes.

Her mother challenged Neel, "So what is your favourite Bengali classic then?"

Neel replied without hesitation, "*Khirer Putul.*"

Nita almost choked on her cookie. Their parents knocked on their ears to make sure that they'd heard correctly. Neel had named a book that was meant for children.

"You haven't read any classics for adults after that?"

Neel wasn't enjoying the turn of conversation.

"Yes, I have read many. But *Khirer Putul* is one book that I reread often," he explained.

Clueless as to how to switch the topic of conversation away from himself, Neel turned to Gita for help. He really didn't understand why they were so gobsmacked by his reading choices.

Gita tried, "Ma, it's a wonderful book. I love it too."

Her rude parent continued as if Neel wasn't sitting right there with them.

"But he should be reading books for grown ups at his age."

"Umm... I read books for all ages," Neel tried to put a word in.

Gita put an end to it with the wise words, "He reads what brings him joy as everyone should do, alright?"

PART 3

Nita's husband called. He was on his way home from the airport and wanted to know if Gita would be there to greet him at the door. He was used to constant attention from his wife. If he didn't get it, he got cranky and stopped buying her gifts for a while.

"Yes, I'll leave the cafe right now," she told him, scraping back her chair.

"Isn't Lily coming to pick you up? She has the car and driver with her at the salon, right?"

"Yes, Ma. I'll just see if she's done," Nita said, putting her phone to her ear.

Neel sighed loudly. He was an introvert. He was dying to get home and recharge his batteries. Gita was tired. She needed a glass of wine and cuddles under a blanket for two. She sprang up to make sure she was wide awake, telling Nita she would just go get her cake from the kitchen.

Nita narrowed her eyes at her.

"Cake?"

"Yes, to take home for the kids."

Nita stared at her sister. Gita wondered if she'd grown horns or a Rudolph like nose.

"You didn't know that Lily is off sugar?"

No, she didn't know. Plus, it was Christmas. Who skipped festive goodies?

Nita thanked her for the thought, adding, "She won't touch anything but apples and kale."

Neel spoke up.

"Apples and kale are great but shouldn't she be eating other things too?"

Eyes tearing him to shreds, Nita growled, "You're young enough to be my child. Don't teach me how to parent my daughter!"

Gita joined in.

"He's right though. She needs all food groups."

Their mother shrieked, "No fish? She's a Bengali girl. Her skin will get dull! Nobody will marry her then!"

Their father wanted the absurd conversation to stop so he could talk books and England with Neel. He shouted out with glee, "Look! Lily has come."

Lily walked in after Neel opened the door for her. Her hair was shiny and her pale cheeks were bright pink with blush. Kohl lined eyes like her mother's scrutinised the room. She said hello to everyone she knew, stopping at Neel's turn.

"Are you my aunt's boyfriend?"

"Yes, he is." Gita answered.

Lily tossed back her hair, throwing a polite smile at Neel. Then she hugged her aunt.

"You're so cool, auntie. Baba has all the fun and Ma just spends her time crying," she told the onlookers who all visibly flinched.

Nita's face turning as red as a tomato, she grabbed Lily's arm and dragged her to the door.

"Enough. Let's go," she hissed, practically pushing her daughter out onto the sidewalk.

Lily waved goodbye to her relatives and Neel. Her grandparents didn't wave back. They looked like they needed a hug.

Neel excused himself to allow them some recovery time. Gita was cool as a cucumber. She'd suspected such things for years when she'd observed her brother-in-law's body language with other women. In fact, Nita had once cried about an affair to their mother who'd kept it a secret from their father. Gita only found out because she'd caught her mother sobbing.

Wiping a tear, Gita's mother spoke. Gita handed her a napkin.

"Lily knows too then," the older woman said with dread.

Gita's father was confused. He asked the women what was being referred to. He could never see his perfect son-in-law in a bad light, so he was doing his best to play dumb. But that wouldn't work today.

"You heard our granddaughter. Did you not?"

"Oof! She's just a child. She was just being silly."

Gita wished Lily had stayed quiet -- especially on a festive day. Pouring water for her parents, she forced a smile. They didn't reciprocate. Her mother just kept on shaking her head in a mix of disbelief and shame.

"I have been a terrible mother."

"No, Ma. It isn't your fault."

She sniffled out, "But I always thought her life looked perfect in everyone's eyes, so I told her to never even think about leaving the bastard."

The distraught woman held her head in her hands, sobbing now. Gita felt tears form in her own eyes. It wasn't nice to see a parent crying. Gita's father put his palm on his wife's shoulder, consoling her softly.

"It's never too late to change our wrong ways of thinking," he told her.

Standing up, he stretched. He'd been sitting for a while so the arthritic pain was nagging at his back. After a good stretch, he made a phone call. It was to his perfect, unhappy daughter Nita.

"Nita. Forgive us. Our home is open for you. And the kids. If you wish to leave him, we will welcome you with open arms."

His voice shook.

Gita wondered if the festive atmosphere was making them extra emotional that day. She went to the back office to see what Neel was up to. He was reading on the ebook reader.

"Can I come out now?"

"I'm so sorry about all this," Gita frowned.

Neel put his ebook reader back in its sleeve. He got up to rub her shoulders. She closed her eyes, sinking into relaxation mode almost immediately. Neel's touch was magic.

"You don't have to be sorry. I expected drama today as you'd warned me already, my love. And I feel bad for your parents," he admitted.

She loved that Neel was full of empathy. Many boyfriends would have ran away after everything he was witnessing including the little boy jibes. Taking his hand, she felt better as they returned to her parents.

The older couple were putting on their sweaters and shawls, in a major hurry. Gita noticed that her mother's hands were shaking.

"Where are you going?" She asked them with surprise.

"To bring your sister home."

Neel offered to drop them but they took a cab instead. Gita hoped for a happy ending for her sister as she waved goodbye to her parents. Rude and bitter Nita hadn't changed Gita's heart. She wished her sister happiness and peace. Hopefully this Christmas would be a new beginning for her.

PART 4

Cafe doors locked again and shutters half pulled down, Gita and Neel were prepared to savour their alone time after all the activity in the last two hours. Gita plopped down on a chair while Neel finished the remnants of his gingerbread cookie. The silence was bliss.

"Well, that went alright I guess," he opined.

Gita made a face, sitting up straighter. "Yes, quite alright."

She remembered something. It was time to stop worrying about her sister and her parents. She had spent most of her life thinking and worrying only about them but she wasn't going to ruin Christmas Eve for herself or Neel.

"So can I open the gift now?" She was not a patient person when she wanted something done.

He nodded, going back to get it. She took out his gifts while he was gone. Handing her the box, he asked her if he could open his gift first.

"Why?" She was very curious.

"Just like that," he gave her a mischievous smile, shoving his hands into his pockets.

Her eyes twinkling, Gita suggested that they open their gifts at the same time. He thought it was a good idea.

All fired up, Gita declared, "On the count of three, okay?"

Neel nodded. Their fingers poised on their respective boxes, the counting commenced.

"One..."

Neel urged her to go faster.

"Two..."

"Stop being so slow on purpose," he said mock angrily.

"Three!"

Neel loved his coffee and Christmassy mugs. But Gita was too overjoyed with her gift to witness his merriment. Neel had given her a pretty necklace with a locket that resembled a slice of cake. Gita loved cake. To be specific, she was crazy about the cake her staff made -- the one with a cherry on top. The locket looked exactly like that cake.

"Thank you," she kissed him, wrapping her arms around him. He held her close, exploring her mouth with his tongue until they both had to stop to catch their breath.

Gita let him put on the necklace for her. After that, she said, "I'll put the box away and we can go to your bed. I mean, your house."

Neel clutched her hand. He took the box from her.

"Don't throw it away yet," he requested.

Gita twirled around, a questioning look on her face. Her lipstick was smeared around her lips and she needed to brush her hair but he soaked in her prettiness. And then he told her there was another gift inside the box.

Gita couldn't believe it. She took the box from him, opening it to find nothing but fragile white tissue at first.

"Are you sure?"

"Yes, I am. Stop being lazy and find it," he chuckled.

Gita giggled as her hands went through the tissue paper. Her gift was a small folded piece of paper in the shape of a heart. It was a precious note. She read it and re-read it while Neel's eyes remained glued to her face. He was waiting with as much anticipation as a man with a marriage proposal. And it was not a marriage proposal, of course.

His note was a proposal of another kind. He was asking the love of his life to share his home with him. No legal bond necessary. No pressure to show the world they were committed to each other. It was just a proposal based on pure love and loyalty.

Gita was speechless as the words went straight to her heart. Simple and direct, Neel's note was perfect although he wished he was a better writer.

I love you, Gita.

Will you share my home with me?

Will you share my coffee machine and my toaster with me?

Will you sleep in my arms every night and wake up next to me?

Please move in with me?

P.S. If anyone calls you a sinner or a cougar, I'll deal with them.

Gita hugged the note to her chest. She was crying. Neel got his answer without any delay. She was sure. She had never been this sure about anything else before, other than opening her cafe.

"Yes, I'll move in with you. And I'm okay with living

in sin if it's with you," she beamed.

Gita and Neel left the cafe hand in hand. No words were said until they reached his home and he handed her the key to what was now *their* home.

"I love you, Gita."

"I love you, Neel."

"Merry Christmas, my love."

"Merry Christmas. Now let's get the wine," she replied.

THE END